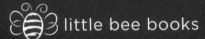 little bee books

251 Park Avenue South, New York, NY 10010
Copyright © 2019 by Little Bee Books
All rights reserved, including the right of
reproduction in whole or in part in any form.

Library of Congress Data
Names: Mae, Jamie, author. | Hartas, Freya, illustrator.
Title: First class / Jamie Mae; Freya Hartas.
Description: First edition. | New York, NY: Little Bee Books, [2019]
Series: Isle of Misfits | Summary: Gibbon the gargoyle is taken to an
island where restless creatures like himself attend school to learn how
to be proper monsters, protectors, team players, and good friends.
Identifiers: LCCN 2018016025 (print) | LCCN 2018024700 (ebook)
Subjects: | CYAC: Gargoyles–Fiction. | Animals, Mythical–Fiction. |
Monsters–Fiction. | Friendship–Fiction. | Schools–Fiction.
Classification: LCC PZ7.1.M29 (ebook) | LCC PZ7.1.M29 Fi 2019 (print)
DDC | [Fic]–dc23 | LC record available at https://lccn.loc.gov/2018016025

For more information about special discounts on bulk purchases,
please contact Little Bee Books at sales@littlebeebooks.com.

Manufactured in China RRD 0520
ISBN: 978-1-4998-0821-6 (pbk)
First Edition 10 9 8 7 6 5 4 3
ISBN: 978-1-4998-0822-3 (hc)
First Edition 10 9 8 7 6 5 4 3 2 1
ISBN: 978-1-4998-0823-0 (ebook)
littlebeebooks.com

Isle of
MISFITS
FIRST CLASS

by JAMIE MAE
illustrated by FREYA HARTAS

little bee books

CONTENTS

CHAPTER ONE

THE LONELIEST GARGOYLE

Gibbon the gargoyle lived atop the same castle all his life. Gargoyles were meant to protect the buildings they lived on. Sometimes, that meant protecting the people inside those buildings, too. That's what Gibbon was always taught.

But Gibbon couldn't stay still in one place *all* day. Sure, it was what he was *supposed* to do, but it was boring! So Gibbon found something new to do to pass the time: playing pranks on people as they walked by below.

And winter was his favorite season for pranks. Winter meant snowballs.

One snowy day, he saw a man in a suit hurrying by the castle. Gibbon quickly made a snowball in his hands. He held it over the edge and dropped it, watching as it hit the man right on the head.

The man jumped from the shock of the cold snow. A confused look crossed his face when he didn't see anyone around. Holding back laughter, Gibbon rolled another snowball and dropped it on the man. This time, the man yelped and ran off.

"*Gibbon!*" a voice whispered harshly.

He jumped and turned toward the gargoyle speaking to him. Elroy was the leader of the castle gargoyles and almost never broke his silence.

"That's enough," Elroy ordered. "You are too old to be playing pranks on the humans. You need to start taking your post seriously."

"But it's so boring!" Gibbon protested. "We just stand around all day. Even at night, we do nothing! What are we even defending the castle from anyway?"

Elroy did not move, but his eyes glared over at Gibbon. "You need to learn how to work with your team, Gibbon. Your slacking off only makes it harder for the rest of us."

With a sigh, Gibbon looked down at the street. He watched as a group of kids stopped below the castle. One of them picked up some snow and threw it at another. Instead of getting mad, the other kid started laughing and made his own snowball. In no time at all, the kids were in a full-fledged snowball fight!

That's what I want, Gibbon thought. For a very long time, Gibbon watched people's lives from the top of the castle. A lot of them had friends and family and fun, but Gibbon didn't really have any of that. The other gargoyles never wanted to play or laugh. They only wanted to watch the world as it went by.

Maybe if I can get Elroy to play, everyone else will loosen up! he thought.

Gibbon smiled. "Hey, Elroy. Catch me if you can! If you do, I'll sit still and guard the castle the rest of the day!"

With a laugh, Gibbon took off. He climbed down the side of the castle, then darted down an empty street.

Gibbon knew—he just *knew*—if Elroy played with him, he'd understand.

But when he stopped and looked back, he didn't see Elroy. His heart sank.

CHAPTER TWO

DOWN IN THE STREETS

Gibbon stopped walking. Should he go back to the castle? Should he wait a little longer and see if Elroy would follow him?

But the longer Gibbon waited, the more certain he was that Elroy wasn't coming. He hung his head as he started to slink back toward the castle.

Wait a minute, he thought as he stopped and looked around again. *This is the first time I've been off the castle!*

He'd only seen the streets from high above. This was the first time he had come down and walked upon them. Should he really go back?

When he turned around, a man was standing in front of him . . . the same one he had thrown snowballs at earlier!

When Gibbon was up on the castle, humans all looked so *small*, but down on their level, these humans weren't small at all. He was big. Really big!

The man screamed and pointed at Gibbon. *"Wh-what is that?!"*

With a scream of his own, Gibbon ran away. After turning down another, quieter street, Gibbon looked over his shoulder and saw that he was alone. This time, he was glad he wasn't being chased. He slowed down and leaned against a storefront to catch his breath.

Did that human think Gibbon was scary? No way, the human was the scary thing!

I need to get back to the castle, Gibbon thought. There, he could look down at the humans from a safe distance. But when Gibbon glanced around, he didn't know where he was. Having lived his whole life at the castle, he didn't know his way around anyplace else.

Gibbon spun around, hoping to see the castle's towers. When he looked toward the storefront again, he yelled. There was something inside the store staring *right back at him*!

He ran to hide behind a mailbox. He slowly peeked out to see if it was gone. But it wasn't. He saw it again, and this time it was hiding behind a . . . mailbox?

Wait, that can't be right. Gibbon narrowed his eyes at the creature in the window.

He held out a hand and shook it. The creature in the window did the same thing. It was gray and made of stone with two horns coming out of its head. One of its horns was broken in half.

Slowly, he walked out from behind the mailbox. And so did the creature. He walked straight up to it. He was so close, nearly touching it, when . . . *BAM!* He walked right into an invisible wall.

Wait! That's me!

Gibbon frowned as he reached out to touch his half-broken horn. How long had it been like that? Was this really what he looked like? The more he looked at his reflection, the more he realized he didn't much look like the other gargoyles. They were bigger than him, and they all had two full horns.

A sinking feeling formed in Gibbon's chest. He didn't just feel different from the others on the *inside*, he also looked different than them on the *outside*, too.

Even if he looked and felt different, the castle was still the only home he had. When he looked up again to try to find the castle's towers, he stopped. Three gargoyles stood in his path. *Big* gargoyles— even bigger than Elroy.

"Hello, Gibbon. I'm Fitzgerald," the one in the middle said. This gargoyle looked way different than the ones from the castle. He had batlike ears and instead of horns, he had two fangs that curled out of his top lip. And he was HUGE!

"Um, hi?" Gibbon replied curiously. He didn't know there were other gargoyles in the city. Maybe they wanted to be friends? Maybe he could go back to their castle instead of his!

"You've got some explaining to do," Fitzgerald said. "A gargoyle should never leave their post. And a gargoyle should never be seen by humans."

"I didn't mean for the human to see me!" Gibbon groaned. "I was trying to get back to my castle, but I don't know which way it is."

"Oh, Gibbon. You aren't going back to that castle," Fitzgerald said with a chuckle. "We have the perfect place for a restless creature like you."

CHAPTER THREE

ISLE OF MISFITS

The other two gargoyles grabbed Gibbon's arms. Gibbon tried to twist his way out of their grasp, but they were too strong. The next thing he knew, they were all up in the air. They flew high above the city, weaving between skyscrapers.

"Where are we going?" Gibbon asked.
Fitzgerald looked at Gibbon with a sly
smile, but didn't answer.

Was he really in a lot of trouble? Who were these gargoyles? Gibbon felt nervous as they flew out of the city.

From the castle's towers, he could sometimes see the shine of the ocean far away, but this was the first time he was seeing it up close. He watched the waves as the gargolyes flew farther and farther away from land. From his home.

Where could they be going?

After flying all night, Gibbon finally spotted a stretch of land over the horizon. As they flew closer, he saw that the island was shaped like a jelly bean and it contained mountains, a lush forest, and a mishmash of buildings. The buildings circled around a grand castle. It was even bigger than the castle Gibbon had lived on.

"That's home," Fitzgerald said as they turned with the wind and flew down.

Once they landed, the two other gargoyles took off toward the castle. "Our castle was the first building on the island. We have protected it, and the island, for a very long time, but after a while we started to get restless. Like you." Fitzgerald explained.

"What *is* this place?" Gibbon asked.

"We call it the Isle of Misfits," Fitzgerald said. "When we started traveling the world, we saw we weren't alone in our curiosity. Many other restless creatures were misbehaving and revealing themselves to people and causing problems. So we decided to turn our island into a place for these misfits, where they can be safe and learn how to be proper monsters. And protectors."

"So, I'm a misfit?" Gibbon asked. His attention drifted from Fitzgerald to two nearby buildings. They were made of wood and had a lot of windows on them. It looked like the top of each building had a garden. Vines wrapped around the sides of the buildings.

"Yes, you are. I've heard about you and your pranks. Once you left your post at the castle, I knew we had to bring you here. You will learn our rules and how to uphold them. One of the most important rules is: *Never be seen by humans*. You've already broken that rule, Gibbon."

Gibbon fidgeted and looked away. "But I didn't know it was a rule!"

"That's why you're here. We'll teach you all there is to know."

"What happens when I learn all the rules? Do I get to go home?"

"If you want. Or you could stay here and go on missions to help other monsters," Fitzgerald said. He waved his hand out toward the rest of the island. "There is a lot to see here. I think you'll like it."

Gibbon looked past Fitzgerald and saw a group of monsters burst out of an old stone building. They were carrying books and backpacks as they walked out of the building. There were so many different kinds of monsters, Gibbon could hardly believe his eyes!

He had only ever seen other gargoyles, but on nights when he had crept into the castle library, he read books about other types of monsters and pored over the pages with pictures, not knowing if they were even real.

Some of the students were in groups, laughing together. Maybe . . . maybe Gibbon could find friends here? At the thought of it, he got so excited, he couldn't stay still.

"I'll give you a tour," Fitzgerald said. He pointed to the smaller buildlings first. "These are where most of your classes will be held. And over there," he pointed toward the wooden buildings with the gardens on top, "are the dorms."

Gibbon nodded eagerly. Near the dorms, he saw a green troll, a hairy gremlin, a slimy ghoul, and a baba yaga, all laughing at a griffin. The griffin was trying to fly, but each time it took off, it veered side to side before falling back down to the ground. It made them laugh even louder.

At first, Gibbon thought it was funny, too. But when he saw how sad the griffin looked, he realized the griffin wasn't playing a game. The griffin really couldn't fly and the others were making fun of it. He was about to go over and say something when Fitzgerald placed a hand on his shoulder.

"Come on, Gibbon," Fitzgerald said. "I'll show you to your dorm room. Tomorrow, you start class."

Inside the dorm, it was bright and airy from all the open windows. A staircase wound up, leading to floor after floor of rooms. As they walked up the staircase, a tiny, sparkly thing flew past Gibbon's head.

"Whoa! Please watch where you're flying, Fiona!" Fitzgerald called out.

"Sorry, boss!" Fiona shouted back.

"What was that?" Gibbon asked as they stopped on the third floor.

"A fairy. I know it might seem overwhelming right now, but you'll adjust. Ah, here is your room! I'll leave you to get settled in," Fitzgerald said as they arrived at a door.

When Fitzgerald opened the door, Gibbon rushed through.

Speechless, he waved goodbye to Fitzgerald before turning his attention back to the room, which had two of everything: two bookcases, two desks, two beds.

"Hi!" came a voice. He turned and saw a dragon who was almost too tall for the room. As the dragon came over, he ran into a dresser and then right into a bed. Gibbon cringed as a shiny red box was knocked off one of the desks and popped open. Gems fell out of the box and spilled everywhere.

"Oops! My treasure!" The dragon bent down to pick them up, but kicked a few away instead.

What a clumsy dragon, Gibbon thought. He knelt down to pick up the shiny rocks that had rolled closer to him and handed them to the dragon.

"Thanks!" the dragon said. "I'm Alistair."

"I'm Gibbon." In comparison to Alistair, Gibbon felt really tiny. As tiny as the fairy that flew by him on the staircase.

Alistair piled his things on the desk before holding out his claw for Gibbon to shake.

Gibbon eyed his claws—they were sharp and long—and wasn't sure if he wanted to touch them.

Alistair frowned and let his arm drop to his side. "I haven't had a roommate all year. I'm happy to have you! It's been a little lonely. Hey, do you want to go to the cafeteria? It's pizza night!"

"Sorry, I'm really tired," Gibbon said as he went over to the open bed.

The island was filled with so many different types of monsters Gibbon had never seen before and it seemed crazy that now he was going to school with all of them.

After traveling all night, the tiredness and shock finally caught up to Gibbon. He just wanted to rest so he could think all of this through.

He could make friends tomorrow, Gibbon decided. Today, he needed to sleep and prepare for his new life on the island.

CHAPTER FOUR

FIRST CLASS

The next day, Gibbon woke to a loud noise. Alistair sat among a pile of books and schedules.

"Sorry! Fitzgerald sent these over while you were sleeping," Alistair explained.

"Thanks," Gibbon said as he picked up a schedule with his name on it and looked it over. On the back, there was a map of the island with each of the buildings marked so he would know where to go.

"We're in the same first class, so I'll show you where it is. It's out in the field where we have all our PE classes. Let's go, we're gonna be late!"

Gibbon tumbled out of bed. He didn't want to be late on his very first day! They gathered up their school books and rushed out of the dorm.

Alistair led Gibbon to a big field in the center of the island. Objects were all around the field, kind of like a maze, but Gibbon wasn't sure what they were for.

"Welcome to PE," the teacher said. Because they got to class late, they were in the very back. It was hard for Gibbon to see over all the creatures in front of him.

"I'm Mr. Dimas and I will be your teacher this year." Gibbon didn't understand why Mr. Dimas was a teacher here. He looked like a normal human. That was until he started walking and Gibbon saw the bottom half of him—he was half horse! *A centaur,* Gibbon realized. He had read about them, but never seen a real, live one. *Wow!*

"For our first class, we'll be working on an obstacle course. It's important to learn how to think fast and work with a team. Everyone, get into groups!" Mr. Dimas ordered.

"Did you see that? He's a centaur!" Gibbon turned toward Alistair, but Alistair was gone. Everyone had quickly gathered into groups. Now he was the only one standing by himself.

Everyone else already has friends, I guess, he thought sadly. The group closest to him looked familiar. It took him a minute to remember they had been the ones laughing at the griffin yesterday. Maybe they weren't actually mean?

He decided to be brave and go say hello. "Hi, I'm Gibbon! Today's my first day here."

The hairy gremlin looked over and narrowed her eyes. "So?"

"Look at his broken horn!" the ghoul said with a laugh.

The troll squinted its eyes. "And you're so small."

"Go away, tiny gargoyle," the baba yaga said.

They laughed at Gibbon as he walked away with his tail dragging behind him. Even surrounded by other monsters, Gibbon still felt alone.

"Why don't you join us?" someone said. Gibbon looked up to see a yeti with so much hair, Gibbon couldn't see his face.

"I'm Yuri," the yeti said. "We could use one more monster."

"Thanks!" Gibbon said as he looked at the rest of the group. Alistair was there, along with the griffin that couldn't fly, and a very angry-looking fairy.

CHAPTER FIVE

ON YOUR MARK, GET SET, GO!

Gibbon didn't think the obstacle course looked too hard. There was a net to crawl under and a tree to climb up, followed by a tall wall to scale using a rope, a series of poles to maneuver through, and at the very end, a track to sprint down to get to the flag.

"The first team to grab the flag wins," Mr. Dimas explained after he walked the groups through the obstacle course. "Now, everyone decide which team member will do each part of the course."

"We should introduce ourselves. I'm Ebony," the griffin said to Gibbon. Her voice was soft and nice.

"You know me already."
Alistair smiled and gave
Gibbon a thumbs-up.

"Fiona," the fairy muttered.

Gibbon was surprised. She
was small and sparkly, so he
had expected a happier voice
to come out of her. Instead,
she sounded grumpy and
had a serious frown
on her face.

"Who are those guys?" Gibbon asked as he nodded toward the other group. The baba yaga barked orders to her teammates, telling each of them where to go.

"Don't mess it up!" the baba yaga ordered. "We have to win!"

"They're . . . not very nice," Alistair said.

Yuri nodded. "Avoid them if you can."

"They're the top students in our class. Always get the highest grades on tests. Always winning competitions," Ebony said with a sigh.

"Won't be winning any personality contests, though," Fiona added.

Gibbon chuckled. He had a feeling he was really going to like it here.

Gibbon was up first. He was so excited to show the team what he could do.

"On your marks, get set, *go*!" called out Mr. Dimas.

The first obstacle was the net that had to be crawled under. He got on his belly and started to crawl and the grumpy ghoul next to him did the same. Gibbon was almost the first one finished when one of his horns got caught in the net.

"Argh!" Gibbon cried out as he struggled to break free. The ghoul laughed at him as he slid out from under the net.

Gibbon finally broke free. Embarrassed, he ran to the tree. He had to make up for that!

"What are you doing? *I'm* supposed to be next!" Alistair called out after him.

Instead of tagging Alistair's hand, he jumped off the ground and flew quickly up the tree as the hairy gremlin was weaving her way up. The gremlin was very fast and Gibbon couldn't catch up to her.

She got to the top first, freeing the rope and throwing it down to the baba yaga.

No! Gibbon finally made it to the top. He started to fly over to the next obstacle, the wall.

"No flying over the wall, you have to climb it with the rope!" Mr. Dimas called out to Gibbon.

Gibbon circled back to the rope in the tree, using it to climb over the wall.

"Wait, you were supposed to give it to me!" Yuri shouted.

"It's okay, I can do this!" he said to Yuri.

Gibbon looked around to see how the other teams were doing. He was shocked. Almost *all* the other teams were ahead of him now. What would happen if he came in last? Would everyone hate him?

I'll have no friends! I can't let that happen!

The next part of the obstacle course was a real challenge. He had to be quick and careful.

As much as he tried to avoid them, he bumped into nearly all the poles as he went through. By the time he got out, the flag at the end of the track was gone.

The troll was holding the flag. His team was laughing and patting each other on the backs as the rest of the students gathered around to cheer them on. When they saw Gibbon, the ghoul grinned and pointed right at him.

"Loser," he said.

Gibbon walked back to his team with his head down. He was so sure he'd win. When he looked up, he saw them glaring at him.

"What was that? We're supposed to work together," Fiona snapped. "Now, we lost!"

"That wasn't cool, Gibbon," Ebony said.

Yuri and Alistair only shook their heads as they left.

CHAPTER SIX

A DIFFERENT KIND OF OBSTACLE

Alistair ignored Gibbon all night. He even left for class all week without him. It made Gibbon feel even more alone to walk to class by himself.

"Hey, little guy," the baba yaga said. Gibbon turned around to see the slimy ghoul with the baba yaga. "We were never introduced. I'm Lissa."

"And I'm Gashsnarl," the ghoul said.

"Hello. I'm uh, Gibbon," the gargoyle responded.

"Did you hear about the obstacle course challenge at the end of the week?" Gashsnarl said. "The team that wins gets their very own mission."

"That's right! But don't get your hopes up. We're going to win." Lissa said with a big grin.

"Yeah, we always win," Gashsnarl said, high-fiving Lissa.

"You and your friends shouldn't even bother trying," Lissa said.

"That's not true! We're going to win, just wait and see!" Gibbon declared.

Now all he had to do was convince them that he could be a team player.

Gibbon had to find the others. This would be the perfect way to make up for his mistake earlier. This time they'd do it together, as a team. And they'd win. Maybe once they won, they wouldn't be mad at him anymore.

And they would get to go on a mission! Going on a mission meant he could see the world—he'd see more than just his castle and the island. *Not only that, but see the world with friends*, Gibbon thought. Nothing would be more fun than that!

He found them at a table in the corner of the cafeteria.

"Hey, guys," he said nervously.

Yuri moved so that he took up the rest of the bench, leaving no room for Gibbon to sit down.

"Yuri, that's not nice," Ebony said softly.

"We lost because of him," Yuri said.

"We didn't just lose," Fiona added, "we came in *last* place!"

"I'm really sorry about doing the course myself, guys," Gibbon said. "I thought if I did well, you guys would want to be my friends. I guess . . . I'm not very good at working on a team. Back home, no one ever wanted to do anything with me, so I was always by myself. I know I messed up yesterday. I'm really sorry."

"You didn't have to win all by yourself to become our friend," Ebony said.

"Yeah, *seriously*. If you wanted to be friends, all you had to do was ask. Duh!" Fiona shook her head.

"Really?" Gibbon asked, surprised. "That's all it would take?"

Yuri scooted over so Gibbon could sit down with them.

"Did you guys hear about the obstacle course challenge next month?" Gibbon asked.

"Of course. We already signed up for it," Alistair said.

"Oh," Gibbon mumbled.

"Why should we let you back on our team?" Yuri asked. "How do we know you won't pull the same stunt as yesterday?"

Gibbon frowned. "I've never really been part of a team before. But I get it now. How we have to work together. Can I . . . can I *please* be a part of your team? Please?"

Ebony looked at her friends. "He said 'please.' "

Alistair sighed. "It's not easy being new here, guys."

Yuri nodded.

Fiona rolled her eyes, but nodded, too.

CHAPTER SEVEN

A SECOND CHANCE

Every day after school for weeks, the five of them trained on the practice course. Yuri was good at deciding what obstacle each of them would do best with the skill they had, even though his hair kept him from seeing very well.

"Why don't you tie your hair up?" Gibbon suggested. "I've seen the really hairy humans do it! I think they call it a 'man bun'?"

"I think it's a good idea! I have some ribbon." Ebony pulled a blue ribbon off her backpack and handed it to Yuri.

"If you guys are sure," Yuri said uncertainly. He tied his hair up into a bun. It was the first time Gibbon could see his eyes—they were ice blue. "Wow! This does make a big difference!"

"Are you guys ready for the challenge?" Alistair asked as he landed next to them. "It's almost time, we should head over."

Everyone nodded. But as soon as they got there, Gibbon's heart sank. The obstacle course looked completely different than the practice one! They had spent all that time training for nothing.

"Uh-oh! It's not the same!" Ebony fluttered her wings in a panic.

"Oh, great, just great," Fiona grunted.

"Let's stay calm, guys," Yuri said.

Unlike the last course, this one started with a tube you had to crawl through. Then there was a seesaw that you had to carefully walk across. After that, there were zigzag balance beams over a mud pit. Next, there was a net wall to climb over. Last, there was a fence to jump over before someone could grab the flag.

"This is totally different," Alistair said as he chewed on his claws. "What are we going to do now?"

"I've got an idea," Yuri said as he huddled everyone together. "Okay, so here's the plan. . . ."

"On your marks, get set, *go*!"

Mr. Dimas blew his whistle.

Ebony was up first. She couldn't fly very well, but she was great at crawling through tubes. She was out first and slapped Fiona's hand.

Fiona delicately walked across the seesaw. Thanks to how tiny she was, the boards barely moved under her weight, which made it easier for her to keep her balance than the other creatures.

She jumped off the other side and high-fived Yuri.

Carefully, Yuri edged his way along the zigzag balance beams. At the final turn, he wobbled so much, Gibbon thought he was going to fall, but he caught his balance at the last second and high-fived Alistair.

Alistair was nearly as big as the net wall, so scaling it was easy for him. The troll from the other team was close behind!

Alistair jumped down from the wall and high-fived Gibbon.

The gargoyle ran as fast as he could to the fence, then jumped over it.

He only had a small ways to go before he could grab the flag, but he was neck and neck with Lissa.

He was so close! *CRASH!*

Gibbon went tumbling down. He looked up and saw the baba yaga smirking as she grabbed the flag.

No! He sat on the ground and held his head in his hands. *I was so close!*

CHAPTER EIGHT

AND THE AWARD GOES TO . . .

They had almost won the race, only to lose at the last second. How could he let this happen?

"What's wrong?" Ebony asked.

"I'm so sorry," Gibbon said. "I lost it for our team."

"Are you kidding me?" Yuri said as he came over. He patted Gibbon on the shoulder. "We came in second!"

"*Second!*" Alistair shouted. "We got *second place*!"

"We've never done that before!" Fiona said. Even she was smiling.

"You're . . . happy?" Gibbon asked as he looked up at the group. "Really?"

"We almost always end up in last place. What's not to be happy about?" Ebony asked with a grin.

Alistair held his claw out to Gibbon. "Come on, friend. It's okay."

Gibbon smiled as he took Alistair's claw and stood up. *Friend.* Gibbon looked from Ebony to Fiona to Yuri, then to Alistair. He had friends.

And that felt even better than winning.

Lissa, Gashsnarl, and the rest of their team stood up on a stage with Mr. Dimas and Fitzgerald. Gibbon wasn't looking forward to watching them gloat.

Mr. Dimas whispered something to Fitzgerald. Fitzgerald nodded and looked out into the crowd.

"Will Alistair, Gibbon, Ebony, Fiona, and Yuri please join us onstage?" Fitzgerald asked.

Gibbon jumped from surprise at hearing his name. He looked to his friends, who also had wide eyes.

"*Us*?" Alistair whispered.

They all walked up onstage together. Gibbon felt awkward being up there with all the other monsters watching him, so he hid halfway behind Alistair, grateful that his roommate was so big.

"What's going on?" the hairy gremlin asked angrily.

"They don't deserve to be up here with us," snapped the troll.

"Of course they do," Fitzgerald replied. "Because *they* are the winners."

"WHAT?!" Lissa shouted.

"I saw you trip Gibbon at the end," Mr. Dimas said to Lissa. "Winners don't cheat. You are hereby disqualified."

The other teams gasped.

"We won?" Ebony said. "Really?"

"Yes, really." Fitzgerald turned to them with a big smile. "I'm very proud of all of you for learning to work so well together. That's exactly why we are here. I'm glad to see you have found some friends, Gibbon."

Gibbon smiled and nodded. He was happy to have friends now and a new place to call home.

"I was going over this mission and well, I think it would be perfect for your team and your . . . unusual set of skills," Fitzgerald said, looking at each of them.

"We get the mission?" Fiona asked.

Fitzgerald smiled. "Only if you want it. So, what do you say? Are you ready?"

They all looked at each other in amazement. "We're ready!"

Isle of
MISFITS
THE MISSING
POT OF GOLD

by JAMIE MAE   illustrated by FREYA HARTAS

READ ON FOR A SNEAK PEAK
FROM THE SECOND BOOK IN THE
ISLE OF MISFITS SERIES!

CHAPTER ONE

READY TO ROLL

When Gibbon and his friends earned their very first mission to help another creature in trouble, he didn't think it would start with them in a classroom. Gibbon tapped his claw against his desk as he waited for the professor to arrive.

Ebony, of course, sat in the very front of the room. She eagerly arranged her colorful pens and notebooks on her desk. Fiona sighed loudly as she fluttered around, filled with too much energy to stay still.

Alistair and Gibbon sat in the middle, both bored as they stared at the clock. Yuri was behind them, snoring away.

Suddenly, the door burst open. Yuri sat up straight and Fiona darted over to her desk as Fitzgerald entered the classroom.

"You've got a great mission!" he announced as he walked in.

Ebony flipped open one of her notebooks and picked up a pen to start taking notes.

"You're going to Ireland," Fitzgerald explained. "You'll be helping a leprechaun by the name of Declan find his missing pot of gold."

"Leprechauns?" Fiona whined. "Seriously?"

Yuri perked up. "What's wrong with leprechauns?"

"Have you ever *met* a leprechaun?" Fiona muttered.

Yuri shook his head, looking at Gibbon and Alistair. Both of them shrugged.

"Just wait," she grumbled. "You'll see what I mean. Or smell, at least."

"Now, now," Fitzgerald said, "a leprechaun's gold is their whole life savings. If you don't find it, he'll have nothing. You'll have to look for clues, decode their meanings, and piece it all together to figure out what happened. Now if you're all ready, follow me."

Gibbon leapt to his feet. Ireland! A whole new adventure with his friends!

CREATURE GLOSSARY

BABA YAGA – a small, fearsome witch from Slavic folklore

CENTAUR – a half human and half horse

DRAGON – a winged and scaly serpent with a crested head and enormous claws

FAIRY – a magical creature who has the form of a tiny human being and can often fly

GARGOYLE – a humanlike or animal figure carved from stone that appears as decorations on buildings

GHOUL – an evil being of legend that robs graves and feeds on dead bodies

GREMLIN – a small, imaginary creature that is blamed when something goes wrong

GRIFFIN – a mythical animal typically having the head and wings of an eagle, and the body, hind legs, and tail of a lion

TROLL – a dwarf or giant of folklore living in caves or hills, or under bridges that is quite unhelpful to humans

YETI – a creature with human or apelike characteristics reported to exist in the Himalayan mountains

JAMIE MAE is a children's book author living in Brooklyn with her fluffy dog, Boo. Before calling New York home, she lived in Quebec, Australia, and France. She loves learning about monsters, mysteries, and mythologies from all around the globe.

◄———————————►

FREYA HARTAS is a UK-based illustrator specializing in children's books. She lives in the vibrant city of Bristol and works from her cozy, cluttered desk. Freya loves to conjure up humorous characters, animals, and monsters, and to create fantastical worlds and places for them to inhabit and get lost in.

Journey to some magical places and outer space, rock out, and find your inner superhero with these other chapter book series from **Little Bee Books!**

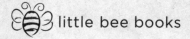

little bee books